The Princess Panda

Tea Party

A CEREBRAL PALSY FAIRY TALE

Story by Jewel Kats

Illustrated by Richa Kinra

Loving Healing Press

The Princess Panda Tea Party: A Cerebral Palsy Fairy Tale
Copyright © 2014 by Jewel Kats. All Rights Reserved.
Illustrated by Richa Kinra

Book #4 in the Fairy Ability Tales Series

Library of Congress Cataloging-in-Publication Data

Kats, Jewel, 1978-
 The Princess Panda tea party : a cerebral palsy fairy tale / story by Jewel Kats ; illustrated by Richa Kinra.
     pages cm. -- (Fairy ability tales)
 Summary: When her orphanage sponsors a tea party competition, an eight-year-old girl with cerebral palsy thinks she has no chance of winning until an enchanted toy panda bear teaches her valuable life lessons.
 ISBN 978-1-61599-219-5 (pbk.) -- ISBN 978-1-61599-220-1 (hardcover : alk. paper) -- ISBN 978-1-61599-221-8 (ebook)
 [1. Cerebral palsy--Fiction. 2. People with disabilities--Fiction. 3. Self-confidence--Fiction. 4. Toys--Fiction. 5. Magic--Fiction. 6. Parties--Fiction. 7. Afternoon teas--Fiction. 8. Contests--Fiction. 9. Orphans--Fiction.] I. Kinra, Richa, illustrator. II. Title.
 PZ7.K157445Pr 2014
 [E]--dc23
                              2014000366

Published by
Loving Healing Press
5145 Pontiac Trail
Ann Arbor, MI 48105
Tollfree USA/CAN 888-761-6268
FAX 734-663-6861

Distributed by Ingram Book Group

For Disability Advocates, John W. Quinn and Michelle Fischer,

Your inspiration is priceless.
Remember, you're the Prince and Princess of your own story...

Michelle stood with her walker *staring*. She'd come to peer at this plush toy over-and-over again at the Salvation Army. Michelle had always feared some other child would take this gem of a stuffed bear home sooner than she.

For this Panda Bear Princess was magnificent.

Her diamond tiara sparkled and twinkled.

Her gently-used silk and taffeta dress held the scent of importance.

Even Panda Bear Princess' paws wore pink sparkly high-heel shoes.

At long last, Michelle was here to claim what she'd been waiting for ever so patiently!

3

Before even daring to touch Panda Bear Princess' toy box, Michelle patted the loose coins in her pocket. Memory told her she had just enough. Michelle let out a sigh of relief. She then gingerly reached for Panda Bear Princess and tucked the toy box into her steel walker's cloth pocket. With rehearsed steps, Michelle paid for her new and only friend at the cash register.

Michelle returned home to her all-girl's orphanage. She was eager to take Panda Bear Princess out of her toy box. As Michelle headed to her accessible bedroom—the only room of its kind in the old red-brick building—she and her walker were stopped in their tracks.

The head mistress, Mrs. Goldsmith, towered over Michelle's eight-year-old rigid frame.

"Stop right there, young lady. Head over to the dining hall right this instant."

Never one to argue, Michelle did as she was asked without saying a peep. All the while, questions about what was going on bubbled through her mind's eye.

Michelle heard a lot of noise coming from the dining hall. Her stomach twisted. She didn't want to see the other girls at the orphanage one bit.

Big, blonde Josephine greeted Michelle at the dining hall entrance door.

The older girl peered at Michelle with ice-cold aqua eyes. "Well, well, look who it is, everyone! Our very own grandmother in residence: Michelle and her unsightly walker!"

Michelle's thin fingers held onto her mobility device extra tight. She could hear laughter pouring out of the room. She continued to walk ahead. Little beads of sweat boiled to the surface upon Michelle's forehead.

Mrs. Goldsmith was already seated inside the dining hall. Even at age fifty, she walked quicker than Michelle.

"Cut it out, Josephine!" Mrs. Goldsmith said loud and clear. "That behavior isn't acceptable. You know Michelle uses a walker because of cerebral palsy."

Sure the laughter had stopped, but Michelle could feel everyone staring at her. She decided to take a seat at the dining table. The ancient table had seen better days. The room was filled with girls from ages five to fifteen. Tension filled the air.

Mrs. Goldsmith now stood up. The room went silent. Eyes of every color looked in her direction.

"You've all been called in here for a very important reason," Mrs. Goldsmith began. She paused, and a rarely seen smile graced her pale face. "The Queen of England is hosting an exchange student scholarship especially for us. Her staff will be here next week to select three girls in a tea party competition. You'll be marked on your grace, manners, and hospitality. The lucky winners will live in London for six months under the Queen Majesty's care."

Michelle felt her bottom sink into her seat, and she heard the other girls in the room shriek.

13

The rest of the meeting occurred in a blur. Michelle wasn't listening. She knew she had no shot at winning, and all she could think about was Panda Bear Princess in her walker's pouch. She was so deep in thought, in fact, that she didn't even notice when the entire dining hall had cleared out.

"You don't look very excited," Mrs. Goldsmith said, breaking into Michelle's thoughts.

Michelle's red curls fell into her face. "I use a clunky walker. I'm the last person with grace," she said in a small voice.

Mrs. Goldsmith sighed. "You have no choice but to participate in the competition. You have from now until next week to get yourself together. There's no ifs, ands, or buts about it," she said sternly.

Michelle felt tears well up in her big, almond-shaped eyes.

Michelle entered her accessible room crying. As always, she was grateful she didn't have to share the large space with any other girl from the orphanage. Michelle sat atop her bed, and she gently pulled out Panda Bear Princess from her walker's pouch. She'd been waiting to open this toy box for weeks, and she never imagined it would happen like this. Michelle fingered the toy. Her heart strings pulled, and out popped a hot tear that plopped onto Panda Bear Princess' felted eye. Right then, right there, Panda Bear Princess's long eyelashes fluttered.

17

Panda Bear Princess stood up in her sparkly pink high-heels. She adjusted the big hair bows behind her ears.

"Gosh! It took you long enough to get me out of that dusty toy box!" Panda Bear Princess started complaining, in an unforgettable high-pitched voice.

Michelle shook her head. This stuff only happened in the movies.

"Are you just going to stare at me, Michelle?" Panda Bear Princess said annoyed. "We don't have much time to prepare for this tea party competition!"

"How...how do you know my name?" Michelle questioned. "How did you know about the Queen's scholarship?

Panda Bear Princess put her paw on her hip. "I have two working ears, you know. Besides, I house hop. I go around to different homes to help kids out through the Salvation Army."

"Makes sense," Michelle said, in awe of her newfound good fortune. "How will you help me prepare for the Royal competition?"

Panda Bear Princess giggled. "That's the easy part."

In a blink, Michelle's therapeutic riding horse landed in the room. Baxter looked as confused as Michelle.

"I gather you know each other?" Panda Bear Princess questioned.

"Well, yes," Michelle answered. "I go riding with Baxter twice per week. He's part of my therapy program for cerebral palsy."

Panda Bear Princess patted the beautiful horse. The pink pads of her stuffed paw tapped at his sides twice. Just like that, magical wings appeared.

"Now, we need to get this show on the road!" Panda Bear Princess exclaimed. "Come on over, Michelle!"

Michelle made her way to Baxter with her walker.

"Can you climb onto his saddle?" Panda Bear Princess inquired.

"I need some assistance," Michelle said.

Panda Bear Princess gave the young girl a boost like an expert. She then folded Michelle's walker and made it shrink so it could fit into the palm of her paw.

With that done, Panda Bear Princess hopped onto the horse's saddle and sat behind Michelle.

Baxter's magical wings flapped and the three of them flew out the window.

23

The world looked so beautiful from up above. Michelle had been on an airplane once, but this was so different. She could actually touch the glimmering stars.

Panda Bear Princess hugged Michelle extra tight. "Nothing beats this feeling."

Then the most extraordinary castle came into Michelle's focus. It was located in the sky above a puff of clouds.

Michelle and Panda Bear Princess were soon standing outside the accessible castle. They tied Baxter up to the landing station.

Michelle stood with her jaw wide-open. Real rubies and emeralds decorated every corner of the castle.

"Welcome to my home," Panda Bear Princess said. "This is where I rest and relax between helping kids in need."

Michelle took in the fragrance of all the flowers.

"We're going to host a royal tea party of our own today," Panda Bear Princess said. "I'll teach you how to be a great hostess."

Michelle pressed the accessible button that opened the magnificent castle's front doors.

"The orphanage may not have automatic doors, but you can always welcome someone inside with a warm smile," Panda Bear Princess said. "Remember to let your guest walk ahead of you."

"Got it," Michelle said.

"Show your guests where they can hang their jackets—even if you can't do it for them."

Michelle nodded.

"Everything should be prepared before your guests arrive," Panda Bear Princess said.

Michelle's eyes took in the beautiful tea party arrangement. Everything was organized perfectly. There was a hand-painted teapot in the centre of the table with decorated cookies and cakes. There were teacups and saucers with spoons and forks set up in a particular order.

"Every utensil has a 'home' at a tea party table," Panda Bear Princess explained. "There'll be a spoon and fork on either side of your saucer to help you stir and prepare your tea. Then, there will be a dessert spoon in front of your saucer."

Michelle understood completely.

"Is your mouth watering, Michelle?" Panda Bear Princess asked. "Yes, of course!"

Panda Bear Princess giggled. "Good! Mine is too." She gestured with her paw for Michelle to sit down. "Remember to allow your guests to sit before you do. Always serve and offer them everything on the table first before you gobble anything up."

Panda Bear Princess did just that. Michelle felt special.

Michelle couldn't help but feel sad. She tried to hide her face behind her teacup.

"What's wrong, my friend?" Panda Bear Princess asked.

Michelle's eyes looked at her walker. "I can perfect all you've taught me, but I'll never be dainty on my feet."

Panda Bear Princess smiled. "With therapy, you'll walk gracefully with your walker. But you know what? Poise comes from the inside—not out. If you're comfortable with yourself, others will pick up on your confident feel good vibes."

Michelle cupped her face and sighed. "I never feel good about myself."

Panda Bear Princess' paw tapped at Michelle's elbows. "It isn't polite to put your elbows on the table."

Michelle immediately removed them. Her eyes looked down.

Panda Bear Princess put her paw on Michelle's face. "Chin up, and follow me. Remember to tuck your chair under the table quietly."

Panda Bear Princess led Michelle to her grand bedroom. They made their way to an antique vanity table. There were Post-It notes taped all along the beautiful mirror. They had messages written on them in Panda Bear Princess' handwriting.

"Every morning when I'm at home, I come and stand in front of this mirror," Panda Bear Princess explained. "I read positive affirmations to pick me up."

Michelle peered closer. "Like this one says: 'You're beautiful, and don't you forget it!'"

"Yes, that's right!" Panda Bear Princess said. "I didn't believe what I'd written at first, but in time I did."

"Wow!" Michelle said, and she definitely planned to do the same in her bedroom.

37

"We better get back to the orphanage," Panda Bear Princess said.

Michelle agreed.

Together, the new friends went out back to meet Baxter.

He was happy to see them.

As before, Panda Bear Princess assisted Michelle to climb onto the horse's back. She shrank her walker, and off the trio went.

They flew through stars and back to the orphanage in no time.

Michelle knew she had a lot of work to do in the upcoming week. She practiced for the tea party every night after all the other girls went to sleep in the orphanage. Michelle wrote beautiful positive affirmations and stuck them on her mirror. She read them every morning.

At long last, the day of the tea party competition had arrived.

41

Her Royal Majesty's team had come as promised. Girls were taken one-by-one to the orphanage's dining hall and tested in private for grace, manners, and hospitality. Michelle stood tall with her walker when her name was called.

"Break a leg," mean Josephine snickered.

"I'll do much better than that," Michelle replied to the blonde for the first time. "I'll be a powerful young girl who knows putdowns only make the person saying them look bad."

With that said, Michelle went inside and did her test. She remembered every tip and trick Panda Bear Princess had taught her.

43

The next day, the winners' names were announced. To Michelle's shock, she had made the cut. She was going to London to live under Her Majesty's care for six months! As luck had it, Josephine wouldn't be coming along.

Michelle went to her room to tell Panda Bear Princess the good news. The stuffed toy immediately did a happy dance.

"Let's start packing!" Panda Bear Princess said.

"It would be selfish if I took you along with me," Michelle said. "I'm no longer a kid in need. I'm much more confident now."

Panda Bear Princess tapped her foot. "So, what are you telling me?"

"I'm returning you to the Salvation Army in your original toy box," Michelle said. "This way, you can bring magic to another child."

"Will you keep in touch with me?" Panda Bear Princess asked.

"You bet," Michelle said. "Your memory will live in my heart forever. Besides, you can always come visit me, and I promise to be a good hostess."

Michelle winked, and Panda Bear Princess did just the same.

About the Author

Once a teen runaway, Jewel Kats is now a two-time Mom's Choice Award winner and Gelett Burgess gold medalist. For six years, Jewel penned a syndicated teen advice column for Scripps Howard News Service (USA) and *The Halifax Chronicle Herald*. She gained this position through The Young People's Press. She's won $20,000 in scholarships from the Global Television Network and women's book publisher Harlequin Enterprises. Jewel also interned in the TV studio of Entertainment Tonight Canada. Her books have been featured in *Ability Magazine* (USA) twice. She's authored

nine books—six are about disabilities. **The Museum of disABILITY History** celebrated her work with a two-day event. Jewel has appeared as an international magazine cover story four times! Recently, her work was featured in an in-depth article published in *The Toronto Star*. Jewel's work has also appeared as an evening news segment on WKBW-TV and on the pages of *The Buffalo News* and *The Huffington Post*.

Please visit her online at **www.jewelkats.com**

46

Cinderalla's Magical Wheelchair: An Empowering Fairytale

Join Cinderella in a World Where Anything is Possible!
In a Kingdom far, far away lives Cinderella. As expected, she slaves away for her cranky sisters and step-mother. She would dearly love to attend the Royal costume ball and meet the Prince, but her family is totally dead set against it. In fact, they have gone so far as to trash her wheelchair! An unexpected magical endowment to her wheelchair begins a truly enchanted evening and a dance with the Prince. Can true love be far behind?

- This fairy tale demonstrates people with disabilities can overcome abuse
- Children with disabilities finally have a Cinderella story they can identify with
- In this version, Cinderella uses her own abilities to build a new future for herself
- The connection Cinderella and the Prince share illustrates love surges past mutual attraction

"An inspiring and exciting read for children of all ages and abilities. Finally here is a book which shows that wheelchair-mobile children can achieve anything. A clever, modern twist on this traditional and much loved story."
--Joanne Smith, TV Producer, *Terry Fox Hall of Fame inductee, Gemini Award winner*

Book #1 in the Fairy Abilities Tales Series from Loving Healing Press
Cinderalla's Magical Wheelchair: An Empowering Fairytale
ISBN 978-1-61599-112-9
Available at Amazon.com, Barnes & Noble, and other children's book retailers

The Princess and the Ruby: An Autism Fairy Tale

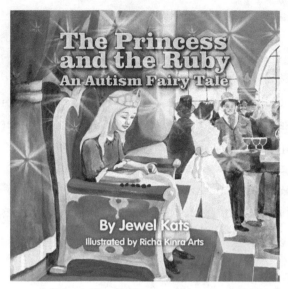

A Mysterious Girl Puts the Future of a Kingdom in the Balance!

One icy-cold winter night, everything changes: a young girl shows up at the king and new queen's castle doorstep wearing little more than a purple jacket and carrying a black pouch. The king recognizes the mystery girl's identity as the long-lost princess without her uttering even a single word. However, the new queen refuses to believe the king's claims. In turn, a devious plan is hatched... and, the results are quite fitting!

- This new twist on Hans Christen Andersen's *The Princess and the Pea* is surely to be loved by all fairy tale enthusiasts.
- *The Princess and the Ruby: An Autism Fairy Tale* adds to much-needed age-appropriate literature for girls with Autism Spectrum Disorder.
- Both fun and education are cleverly weaved in this magical tale, teaching children to be comfortable in their own skin and to respect the differences of others.

"*The Princess and the Ruby* is a heartwarming narrative; a tale that beautifully depicts several unique characterizations of Autism Spectrum Disorder. Jewel Kats has refreshingly shed light upon a daily struggle to redefine 'normalized behaviors', in an admirable effort to gain societal acceptance and respect."   --Vanessa De Castro, Primary Residential Counselor with Autistic Youth

Book #2 in the Fairy Abilities Tales Series from Loving Healing Press
The Princess and the Ruby: An Autism Fairy Tale
ISBN 978-1-61599-175-4
Available at Amazon.com, Barnes & Noble, and other children's book retailers

Snow White's Seven Patches: A Vitiligo Fairy Tale

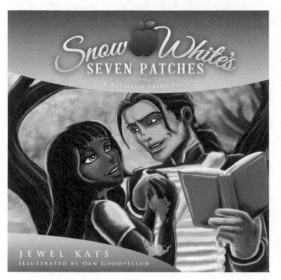

Snow White's Seven Patches: A Vitiligo Fairy Tale is a modern-day story with the classical theme of good conquering evil. You'll find the age-old ingredients of a magic mirror, poisonous apple, dwarfs, and romance here. However, this adaptation includes a vain mother who's so clouded by beauty myths that she keeps her own daughter a secret, while plagiarizing the workings of her mind. Everything falls apart when the good mirror finally speaks the truth.

Young readers with vitiligo will look at their own skin patches with a unique lens, finding interesting shapes and stories behind each puffy cloud of white.

- Readers will be introduced to the firsthand-hurt that plagiarism can cause through Snow White's experience.
- The loving dwarf family illustrates that helping people in need should be a priority in life.
- Readers learn that not all princesses look alike.
- The concept of "beauty is within the eye of the beholder" is exemplified by the prince and magic mirror.

"In *Snow White's Seven Patches*, Jewel emphasizes how to overcome adversity with creativity. She encourages children to maintain a healthy perspective about their physical appearance. Jewel reminds us that despite wickedness, we can move on and get about the business of life."

--Carole Di Tosti, novelist, reviewer for Blogcritics.com

Book #3 in the Fairy Abilities Tales Series from Loving Healing Press
Snow White's Seven Patches: A Vitiligo Fairy Tale
ISBN 978-1-61599-206-5
Available at Amazon.com, Barnes & Noble, and other children's book retailers

CPSIA information can be obtained
at www.ICGtesting.com
Printed in the USA
LVHW062008271118
598428LV00008B/51/P

9 781615 992195